PRESENTED TO

———————————————————

FROM

———————————————————

DATE

———————————————————

I'll Be With You
ALWAYS

WRITTEN BY
JONI EARECKSON TADA

ILLUSTRATED BY CRAIG NELSON

CROSSWAY BOOKS ❧ WHEATON, ILLINOIS

A Division of Good News Publishers

PUBLISHER'S ACKNOWLEDGMENT

The publisher wishes to acknowledge that the text for *I'll Be with You Always* appeared originally in *Tell Me the Promises,* written by Joni Eareckson Tada with Steve Jensen and illustrated by Ron DiCianni. Special thanks to Ron DiCianni for the idea and vision behind the creation of the series. For more stories in the "Tell Me" series, *Tell Me the Story, Tell Me the Secrets,* and *Tell Me the Truth,* all published by Crossway Books, are available at your local bookstore.

I'LL BE WITH YOU ALWAYS
Copyright © 1998 by Joni Eareckson Tada
Published by Crossway Books
a division of Good News Publishers
1300 Crescent Street
Wheaton, Illinois 60187

Illustrations by Craig Nelson
Design by D² DesignWorks
First printing 1998
Printed in China

LIBRARY OF CONGRESS CATALOGING-IN-PUBLICATION DATA
Tade, Joni Eareckson.
   I'll be with you always / Joni Eareckson Tada: illustrated by Craig Nelson.
   Originally appeared in Tell me the promises.
   Summary, A disillusioned artist, who feels his talent will never match that of his father, is restored by the older man's love and faith.
   ISBN 1-58134-000-1
   [1. Fathers and sons—Fiction.   2. Artists—Fiction.   3. Conduct of life—Fiction.]   I. Nelson, Craig, 1947- ill.   II. Title.
PZ7.T116lal   1998
[Fic]—dc21   98-3942

06	05	04	03	02	01	00	99	98

15 14 13 12 11 10 9 8 7 6 5 4 3 2 1

To Cori Bohn

God's hand is on you.

Justin William Chase, Jr.,

leaned around the half-opened door of his father's study.

Actually, it wasn't so much a study as an art studio. And

whenever the hallway smelled like turpentine and oil paint, Justin

could tell that his father was about to begin work on a new painting.

Sure enough, Justin William Chase, Sr., in his long paint-splattered

smock, was turning a large easel in the direction of the sunlight that

streamed through the tall window. Next to the easel was a small table

covered with bottles and brushes, tubes, paint rags, and several palettes.

Justin, who wanted nothing more than to be a famous painter like his

father, saw his chance to have fun.

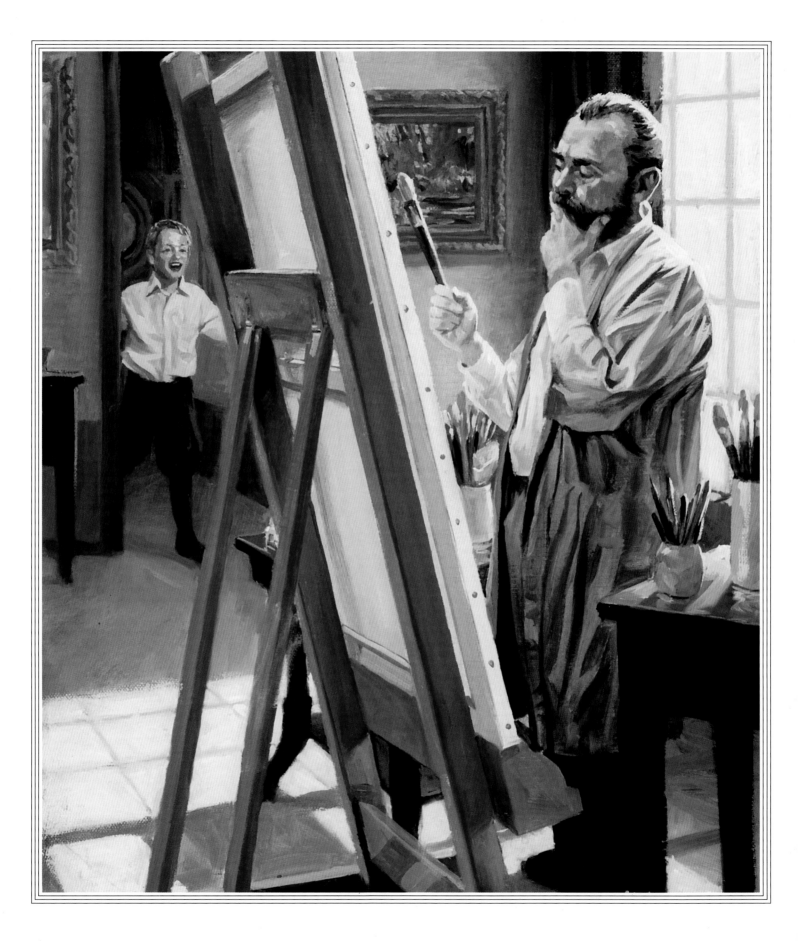

Father," he said as he ran into the room, "may I help you get ready?" Justin reached for a couple of the tubes of paint and began to put them in neat little rows. "Better than that," Mr. Chase said with a smile, "why don't you bring my stool over and sit up here on my knee?" That was exactly what the little boy was hoping his father would say. Within minutes, Justin was doing his favorite thing in his favorite place. He was sitting on his father's lap before a huge canvas in the studio of Boston's most famous artist of the 1800s—his dad. What's more, his dad was letting him paint. Nothing thrilled Justin more than to hold one of his father's brushes. Mr. Chase would then wrap his large hand around Justin's and dab the brush into the paint on the palette. Holding on to his son's hand and the brush, the artist would swirl the most beautiful colors across the canvas. Justin, all wide-eyed and grinning, delighted in feeling his father's hand around his. Even more, he thrilled to see the canvas begin to fill with red and blue and yellow.

He was painting! Actually, his father was doing the painting, but from Justin's point of view, it was hard to tell the difference. He didn't know which was more fun: creating something beautiful right before his eyes or sitting on his dad's knee and feeling the warmth and gentle pressure of his father's hand. The little boy really didn't care. All he cared about was being with his dad and feeling important and safe.

With such care and good training, it was no surprise that within a matter of years Justin William Chase, Jr., went to one of the finest art schools in New England. His teachers were amazed at their young student's talent. Once, while watching Justin angle his brush a certain way on the canvas, one of his teachers remarked, "How did you become so skilled with the brush?" The young man turned and, with smudges of paint on his chin, thought for a moment, looking off in a dreamy way. He said softly, "I can almost feel my dad's hand around mine when I paint." Justin then shook his head, as if coming out of a dream. "My father is getting older, but he's still the best painter in the world. And one day," he added, "I will be famous just like him!" And it was true. His father was very famous—although he cared little about fame and fortune. He simply delighted in being a good painter. The old artist would say to his son, "Justin, don't make fame your goal. Just enjoy the gift God has given you. Paint for Him and give of yourself wherever He places you."

Yes, Father." Justin would nod obediently, but when he was back at school, flipping through art books, and happened to see a page with one of his father's paintings on it, he'd swell with pride. Yes, Justin Chase, Jr., would one day go to Paris to study and become a great painter—a famous painter—like his father. Finally, the day arrived when Mr. Chase stood with his grown son on the Boston docks next to a big steamship about to sail for Europe. Justin put down his suitcases and hugged his aging father. He was surprised at how frail and thin the older man seemed. Justin hated leaving him.

The trip across the Atlantic Ocean took many days. Sometimes on windy afternoons, Justin would walk to the stern of the boat, lean on the ship's rail, and look back toward America. Oh, how he missed his father and how he hoped he was feeling better. Then Justin would walk forward to the bow and feel the wind in his face. He would think about Europe and Paris and attending the best art school in the world. ❦ Paris was even better than he had imagined. Every day he and his fellow students visited museums and galleries or took long field trips out into the French countryside. They would take out their sketch pads at every chance, perhaps stopping by a stream to discuss how to paint the water that gurgled and splashed over rocks. Justin always seemed to have an idea. "I think that since water moves fast," he would say, "you should paint it fast and not be too careful. Like this . . ." And then he would quickly and artfully sketch the stream. It was perfect. His skill did not go unnoticed. Justin was quickly becoming known not only among the students, but among the art experts.

Many letters passed back and forth between Paris and Boston. As time went by, Justin noticed that his father's handwriting was becoming more scribbly and hard to read. But always, somewhere in the letters, the old painter would write, "Son, I believe in you. I am here if you ever need me." Those words always brought a tear to Justin's eyes. He would carefully fold his father's letters and then turn to his art and work even harder. It was this commitment that won Justin such fame among the gallery owners in Paris. And not just Paris, but throughout all of Europe. Well-known art collectors began to seek out the paintings of Justin William Chase, Jr. Justin wrote long letters to his father, explaining that now his works were hanging in the finest palaces throughout all of France and beyond while requests for his paintings were constantly pouring in. But fame and fortune took its toll. "Where is my painting?" demanded a wealthy collector who stormed into Justin's studio one day.

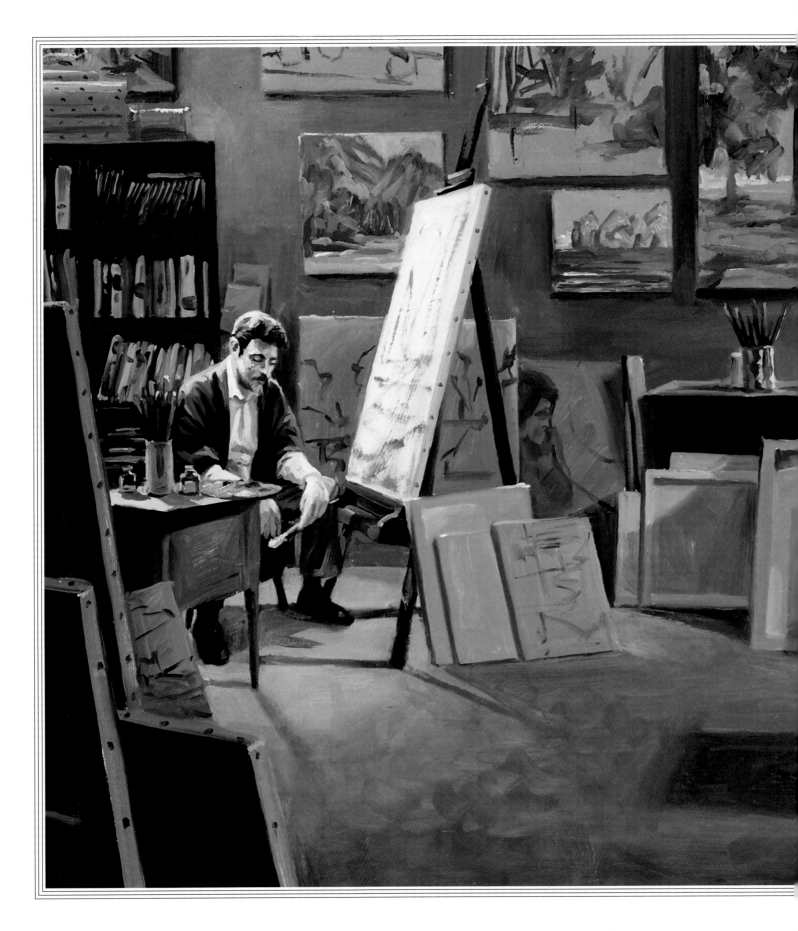

But he had to stand in line. Others were ahead of him asking, "When will you finish my order?" and "I thought you would have my painting framed by now!" Justin could only turn to his work and paint as fast and furiously as he could. He never realized there would be so much pressure and disappointment connected with being famous. Sometimes, in the middle of a painting, he would wonder, *My father was famous, but he was happy. Why am I so sad?*

Back in America, the old painter sensed something wrong. For one thing, there were fewer letters than in earlier days. For another, the art critics were beginning to question the works of the young artist who, as they wrote, "will never be as good as his father." The old artist sighed and sent a message. "My son, come home," and then added with emphasis, "come home before it's too late." When the message arrived, Justin was shocked. "Come home before it's too late," he read. What did this mean? Was his father's health worse? Bewildered, he put the letter down and looked around his studio. There were no longer lines of people asking for his works. Surrounding him were piles of unfinished paintings and blank canvases. He was afraid he would never be able to paint a beautiful painting again. He glanced again at his dad's message, and tears filled his eyes. *I've lost my talent— and now I might lose my father.* The following day Justin booked passage on the next steamship back to America.

Arriving in Boston, Justin hurried home, caught his breath, and then quietly walked into the familiar study. His father, frail and leaning on a cane, sat on his stool near one of the old easels. Sunlight streamed in and bathed the old man in a warm glow. Justin shut the door behind him. "I've been waiting for you," the painter said with a smile. "Oh, Father," Justin cried as he walked over and knelt by the stool. "I'm not too late. You're all right." "Yes, everything's all right. And, my son, it's not too late for you either. I have heard about your work. About your—" "Father, I'm so ashamed. After all these years, I have finally realized that I don't have your gift. I'll never be the artist you are." Justin buried his head against his father's knee. The old painter placed his hand on his son's head. "Dear Justin, I don't care if you are ever famous. I only care that you become all that God intends you to be; and for this, my child, it is not too late. Here. Come with me to my easel."

Justin walked arm-in-arm with his father over to one of the large blank canvases. They stood there for a moment, and then the old man said, "Reach for one of my brushes, son." Justin held the brush up in his hand, and the next thing he knew, his father was standing behind him and had wrapped his thin hand around his. Suddenly he was a child again, feeling his arm lift and stretch as together, under his father's strength, they splashed and dabbed paint on the canvas. It was just two hands on a single brush, swirling and stroking and filling the entire canvas with beautiful color.

Oh, this is wonderful!" Justin laughed out loud. "I haven't had this much fun in years!" In less than an hour, father and son stood before the most beautiful painting Justin had ever seen. "Father, look at what you did. It's amazing! After all this time, you've only gotten better. Do you see this?" He turned to the old man. He paused for a moment and was struck by the way the sun touched his father's face. The golden rays washed away the age and wrinkles, and Justin felt as though he were seeing a side of his father he had never known before. He roused from his thoughts and said one more time, "Father, look . . . do you see what you've done while guiding my hand?" There was a long silence. And then, very slowly, the old painter spoke. "No, Justin, I can't see. I am almost blind. I cannot see the canvas." His son slowly shook his head in disbelief. "How?" he stammered. He turned to the painting. "How did you do this if you can't see?"

Justin, *you* did it. The gift never left you. All you needed to overcome your fear was to feel my touch and to know my presence and love for you—to know *God's* love and presence. Fame—even failure—can make a person forget things like that. This is why I wanted you to come home. It wasn't for my sake." The old man wrapped his arms around his boy. "It was for your sake." Justin held his father as tightly as he could and cried. Not with sad tears or tears of regret, but tears of relief and joy. "Give of yourself wherever God places you," the old artist said as he patted his son's shoulder. His blind eyes became wet, too, when he added, "And remember, for as long as He allows, my hand will always be near to guide you."